WAYANS FAMILY PRESENTS

Amy HODGEPODGE
PLAYING GAMES

BY KIM WAYANS & KEVIN KNOTTS
ILLUSTRATED BY SOO JEONG

Grosset & Dunlap

For Elvira, Howell, Billie, and Ivan.
And for Sylvia—the best teacher ever.

GROSSET & DUNLAP
Published by the Penguin Group
Penguin Group (USA) Inc., 375 Hudson Street, New York, New York 10014, USA
Penguin Group (Canada), 90 Eglinton Avenue East, Suite 700, Toronto, Ontario
M4P 2Y3, Canada (a division of Pearson Penguin Canada Inc.)
Penguin Books Ltd., 80 Strand, London WC2R 0RL, England
Penguin Group Ireland, 25 St. Stephen's Green, Dublin 2, Ireland
(a division of Penguin Books Ltd.)
Penguin Group (Australia), 250 Camberwell Road, Camberwell, Victoria 3124, Australia
(a division of Pearson Australia Group Pty. Ltd.)
Penguin Books India Pvt. Ltd., 11 Community Centre, Panchsheel Park,
New Delhi—110 017, India
Penguin Group (NZ), 67 Apollo Drive, Rosedale, North Shore 0632, New Zealand
(a division of Pearson New Zealand Ltd.)
Penguin Books (South Africa) (Pty.) Ltd., 24 Sturdee Avenue,
Rosebank, Johannesburg 2196, South Africa

Penguin Books Ltd., Registered Offices:
80 Strand, London WC2R 0RL, England

Copyright © 2008 Gimme Dap Productions, LLC.
Published by Grosset & Dunlap, a division of Penguin Young Readers Group,
345 Hudson Street, New York, New York 10014. GROSSET & DUNLAP is a trademark of
Penguin Group (USA) Inc. Printed in the U.S.A.

Library of Congress Control Number: 2008032954

ISBN 978-0-448-44898-5   10 9 8 7 6 5 4 3 2 1

Chapter 1

"Where is everybody?" Lola wondered as she stepped through the front doors of Emerson Charter School and onto the sidewalk.

"What do you mean, 'everybody'?" I joked, pointing to myself and our friends Pia and Rusty. "We're right here."

Lola stuck out her tongue at me. "Very funny, Amy Hodgepodge!"

I laughed, knowing she was only kidding. Lola has a great sense of humor. She's the one who came up with my nickname: Amy Hodgepodge. My real name is Amy Hodges. But when Lola found out that I'm African American, White, Japanese, and Korean, she said my name should be Amy Hodgepodge. Lola and her twin brother, Cole, are mixed-race, too. So are some of my other friends. But Lola says nobody is as mixed as me!

"Brr," I said, wrapping my arms around myself as a brisk autumn wind blew through the bus parking lot. It was chillier outside than it had been that morning. "I hope the others get here soon. I'm freezing!"

Our friend Pia checked her watch. It was pink with little rhinestones on it. Everything Pia wears is always super stylish. "Maybe Mrs. Musgrove held them back," she said. "She's always catching them doing something wrong. It's like she has eyes in the back of her head or something."

The fourth grade at Emerson was divided into two sections. Every time I heard how strict Mrs. Musgrove was, I was even happier that I was in Mrs. Clark's section with Lola, Pia, and Rusty. Lola's brother Cole and our other two friends Jesse and Maya were in Mrs. Musgrove's section.

"Yeah," Rusty added. "Remember how during the first week of school she made Cole sweep her classroom floor just because she saw him drop one candy wrapper by accident?"

Lola and Pia nodded, remembering the story. But I didn't. That's because my family had moved to Dyver City a few weeks after the beginning of the school year. And as if starting school late wasn't hard enough, this was the first time in my life that I was going to regular school. Before our move, I'd been homeschooled by my parents and grandparents. But this year I'd talked my family into letting me try regular school, and so far I loved it.

Just then I heard a shout. I turned and saw Jesse racing toward us.

"Hey, did you guys hear about Danny Kaja?" she asked breathlessly.

"No. What about him?" Pia looked curious. She loves gossip.

Cole was right behind Jesse. "Mrs. Musgrove yelled at him for shooting spitballs," he said.

"Wow." I was surprised. "That doesn't sound like Danny."

"Yeah, he never gets in trouble," Rusty added.

Lola nodded. "He's always so quiet and polite. It's hard to believe he'd shoot spitballs at a teacher!"

"Hey, where's Maya?" Pia peered around Jesse and Cole, looking for our other friend from Mrs. Musgrove's class.

Jesse shrugged. "I thought she was right behind us. She'll probably be here soon."

Just then another gust of chilly wind blew my ponytails around and made me shiver. "Let's wait for her on the bus. It's pretty cold out here," I suggested.

"We're not taking the bus today, Amy," Lola said.

Pia nodded. "Yeah. It's Monday. We have basketball practice, remember?"

"Oh, right. I forgot." I felt kind of disappointed that I'd have to ride home without my friends. All my girl friends were on a team in the Maple Heights Girls' Basketball League. They practiced several days a week after school. Their team was called the Comets, and it had

❄ 4 ❄

one of the best records in the whole league. Rusty and Cole were on a team in the boys' league, but they practiced on different days.

"My dad should be here to walk us over to the courts any second," Jesse said impatiently. "Maya and Evelyn had better get out here soon!"

Jesse's father was the Comets' coach. He was a firefighter who worked at the fire station a few blocks from our school. On practice days, he came and walked all the league kids from Emerson over to the basketball courts at Sycamore Street Park. There were other coaches who picked up the rest of the kids in the league from their different schools. Then everyone met up at Sycamore Street Park and split up into their teams to practice.

Lola laughed. "Your dad is way more patient than you are, Jesse," she said. "He'll wait if they're a little late."

"I can't believe Evelyn isn't here," Pia said. "Usually she's the first one waiting outside on basketball days."

Evelyn Najera was the star of the Comets. She loved sports—all sports. She was probably the most athletic kid in the fourth grade. She could even beat some of the boys at arm wrestling.

"Hello, hello!" Jesse's dad called as he hurried into sight around the corner of the building.

"Hey, Mr. Edwards," a few of the other kids called.

"Dad, you're late," Jesse informed him. "But don't worry, so are Maya and Evelyn."

"That's okay," Mr. Edwards replied, glancing around. "Looks like we're still missing some of the kids from the other teams, too."

"No problem," Lola joked. "If we leave without them and they can't practice, they'll be easier for us to beat."

Mr. Edwards laughed. Then he noticed me and said, "Well, hello, Amy. Are you coming along to cheer your friends on today?"

"I wish I could," I said. "But I'm supposed to go out to dinner at the Tisdale Street Taqueria with my family tonight. Maybe another day."

"All righty." Mr. Edwards checked his watch. "I'd better go start counting heads and see who's still missing." He hurried off toward some of the other kids who were standing around outside.

"Are you sure you can't come watch us for a little while?" Pia asked. "You had fun when you came to see our game last week, right?"

"Yeah! You guys were great," I said. "But I don't think I have time before dinner."

"Oh, no!" Jesse gasped.

I blinked in surprise. I couldn't understand why Jesse would sound so upset that I was going out to dinner with my family. Did she know something I didn't? Was the food at the taqueria rotten or something?

Just then I realized Jesse hadn't been looking at me. She was staring toward the entrance to the school. Evelyn was just coming out. Her right arm was in a sling!

"Oh my gosh! What happened to you?" Pia cried as Evelyn trudged over to join us.

"I sprained my wrist," Evelyn said sadly. "I

was running though the halls to come meet you guys and I fell."

"Does it hurt?" Rusty asked.

"Only a little." Evelyn grimaced. "The school nurse thinks it's a sprain. She said I probably won't be able to play sports for a whole month. But I've got to get it checked out by the doctor, just in case it's broken. My mom is on her way here now."

Evelyn looked really sad. I guessed that for Evelyn, a month with no sports would be like a month for me without my scrapbooks. Scrapbooking is my favorite hobby. I have an awesome scrapbook I started when my grandmother gave me some really pretty handmade paper. It's filled with photos, drawings, ticket stubs, and other stuff to help remind me of my favorite people, places, and events. I couldn't imagine not working on it for a whole month.

"No way, Evelyn. But that means you're out for the whole rest of the season!" Jesse cried.

Then I heard someone from behind me say, "We heard you're a player down. Too bad. Guess that means you won't be winning any championships this year. Or any games at all."

I glanced over my shoulder and saw Jennifer Higgins standing there smirking at us. Jennifer is tall and blond and pretty and thinks she's perfect. So do her two best friends, Liza and

Gracie. They were standing right beside her.

"Yeah, too bad," Gracie added. "Guess we'll see you guys on the court. If you can still play, that is."

Jesse scowled as the three girls walked away. "Those jerks," she muttered. "They just couldn't wait to come and brag."

I thought I knew why she was worried. Jennifer's team, the Uptown Girlz, was really good. Everyone said the Comets and the Uptown Girlz would probably end up playing each other in the finals this year.

Just then Maya finally came out of the school building and walked over to us. "Hi, guys," she said in her soft voice. "Sorry I'm late."

"Did you hear, Maya?" Jesse cried, gesturing toward Evelyn.

Evelyn caught Maya up, then said, "I'm really sorry. Even if it's just a sprain, I'm definitely going to have to sit out the rest of the season."

"Don't worry, you guys," I said. "You can still beat the Uptown Girlz even without Evelyn."

Lola shook her head. "It's not that simple,"

she said. "Without Evelyn, there will only be seven members left on our team."

"And the league rules say there have to be at least eight," Evelyn added, looking miserable.

"No big deal," Cole said. "You guys just need to find another team member."

"And fast!" Rusty nodded. "Maybe I could put on a wig and play," he joked.

I giggled, but Lola quickly added, "It's not going to be that easy. All the girls who want to join the league would have joined by now. Who would want to start playing at the very end of the season?"

"Like, maybe someone who started school late?" Jesse said with a grin.

All of a sudden everyone turned and stared at me.

"You like basketball, right, Amy?" Pia said.

"Um, sort of." I shrugged. "I like watching it on TV with my grandfather. But I've never really played before."

"It's not that hard," Jesse said eagerly. "You

just dribble and shoot. Easy as pie."

I bit my lip. Before I could answer, Jesse's dad returned. The others immediately told him about Evelyn's wrist and their idea to have me take her place on the team.

Jesse's dad smiled at me. "How about it, Amy?" he said. "I'll call your parents if you'd like to come out today and give it a try. Players

of all skill levels are welcome in the Maple Heights Basketball League. It doesn't matter if you've never played before."

"I don't know," I said slowly.

"Well, why don't you just come and watch today for a little while?" said Mr. Edwards. "Then you can make up your mind if you want to play next time."

"Well . . ." I wasn't sure what to say. It had always been a secret dream of mine to play sports, but I was afraid I was too clumsy to be any good at it. Still, with all my friends staring at me so hopefully, how could I say no? "Okay," I said at last. "I guess I can call my parents and ask."

Jesse's dad took out his cell phone, and I used it to call my mom. After I explained about Evelyn and then asked permission to go to the park to watch their practice, my mom said it was okay.

"We'll swing by and pick you up on the way to the restaurant," she said. "Do you think basketball practice will be over by five?"

"I think so," I said. "Thanks, Mom."

"Come on," Lola cried as soon as I hung up. "Let's hit the courts!"

Chapter 2

Watching my friends play basketball was really different from the games I'd seen on television. My friends and their teammates from St. Victoria's Elementary—Teresa, Taylor, and Emily—did all sorts of cool drills and exercises. It seemed like they didn't stop running the entire time I was there.

"What do you think, Amy?" Lola asked breathlessly, jogging over to where I was sitting. "Do you think you could do it?"

"Most of it, I think," I said uncertainly. "But what's that called when you kind of jump up and grab the ball after someone else shoots it at the basket?"

"You're kidding, right?" Lola laughed. "I thought you said you watched b'ball on TV with your granddad."

I shrugged and smiled. "Usually when I watch sports with him, I'm working on my scrapbooks at the same time," I explained. "I don't always pay that much attention to the game."

"That's sort of how my mom watches sports with my dad, too," Lola said with a grin. "Anyway, that's called a rebound. The kind of

rebound Coach was just having us practice is called a put-back."

"Oh, okay. Thanks." I waved as she jogged back out onto the court. There was a lot to learn about basketball now that I was paying attention. I was impressed by how action-packed it was. My friends never seemed to stop moving! It made me tired just watching them.

The practice was still going on when I saw our car pull to the curb outside the park's chain-link fence. I could see my dad behind the wheel. I waved to let him know I'd seen him, then ran over to tell my friends and Coach Edwards that I was leaving.

"Thanks for coming, Amy," he said. "I hope you'll think about joining our team. We'd love to have you."

"Thanks. I'll think about it," I promised him. Then I said good-bye to my friends and hurried toward the exit.

My mom was sitting in the passenger seat beside my dad. Her parents—my grandparents—

were in the backseat. They live with us. Both of them used to help with my homeschooling before I started going to regular school.

I climbed in next to my grandmother. "How was the sports rehearsal, Little Mitsukai?" she asked. That's her nickname for me. It means "Little Angel" in Japanese.

"They call it a practice, not a rehearsal, Obaasan," I said as I put on my seat belt. "And it was pretty interesting."

My grandfather leaned forward to smile at me. "Your mother tells us you may join the team. Is that right?"

"I don't know." I glanced out the window as the car pulled away from the curb. I could just barely see my friends still practicing inside the park. "I mean, I've never played on a sports team before. And my friends are really good—I'd probably never be able to play well enough to keep up with them."

My dad glanced at me in the rearview mirror. "Don't sell yourself short, Amy," he said.

"You learned to play badminton as part of your homeschooling unit about the Olympics last year, remember?"

"Ah, yes!" my grandfather said. "By the end, she was beating me every time."

I shrugged. Playing badminton with my grandfather wasn't really the same thing as playing basketball on a team. Plus, it took me a while to get good at badminton.

"I guess," I said. "But I'm sure they can find someone better than me to replace Evelyn."

"Well, if you change your mind I'd be happy to practice with you," my grandfather said. "I used to be quite the athlete in my younger years."

As we sat down at the restaurant I couldn't stop thinking about joining the basketball team. On the one hand, it would be fun to try something new and spend more time with my friends. Plus they really needed another person on their team. On the other hand, Evelyn was the best player on the Comets. How could I

possibly replace someone like that? And the last
thing I wanted to do was to let my friends down.

❀ ❀ ❀

I was still thinking about joining the team
as I walked into music class on Wednesday
afternoon. Both sections of the fourth grade
have music together, and the kids from Mrs.
Musgrove's section were already there. Lola,
Pia, and I went over to join Maya and Jesse.

"So are you going to join the Comets?" Jesse
asked me right away.

Pia elbowed her. "Don't be pushy, Jesse," she
said. "She already told you yesterday and this

morning that she hasn't made up her mind yet."

I smiled awkwardly. "Yeah. I'm still thinking about it."

"You know . . ." Jesse said. "Our next practice is today, and our next game is on Monday."

"You heard Pia, Jesse," Lola said. "Leave Amy alone. She'll decide when she decides." Even though Lola was trying to give me some space to make up my mind, she was still smiling at me hopefully.

Our teacher, Mr. Ship, was leaning against the piano at the front of the room. He clapped his hands for attention.

"Good morning, everyone," he said, brushing back his hair with one thin hand. "I hope you're all feeling creative today, because we're about to start a new project."

I was glad that we had a new music project so I could think about something besides basketball for a minute. Music is one of my favorite classes. I've always loved singing, and everyone says I'm pretty good at it.

Mr. Ship told us about the project. We were supposed to divide ourselves into groups. We would have a few weeks to write a song, figure out what instruments we should use to accompany it, and practice performing it. Then at the end of the practice period we would all get to record our songs in a real, professional recording studio that one of Mr. Ship's friends owned nearby.

"This is going to be so amazing!" Jesse exclaimed after Mr. Ship told us to go ahead and choose our groups. "I always thought I had the right kind of voice to be a recording star."

"Too bad you're the *only* one who ever thought it," said Lola with a grin.

Rusty and Cole hurried over. "Want to be a group of seven?" Rusty asked us.

"It'll be like a sequel to our awesome triumph in the talent show," Cole added.

I smiled, remembering the school talent show. The seven of us had won second place for performing a song we wrote together.

"Sounds great," I said as we all gathered around one of the music room's round tables. "Let's start writing down some ideas."

"I'll take the notes if you want," Pia offered. She pulled out her favorite pink strawberry-scented pen.

"Make sure there's a solo for me," Jesse said.

"And a bigger solo for Amy," Rusty added. "She was awesome in the talent show, remember?"

"Maybe Maya can play the xylophone," Cole suggested.

"That sounds like a great idea," I agreed.

"What do you think, Maya?"

Maya didn't answer. I looked over at her. She was staring into space.

Lola noticed, too. "Maya?" she said, standing up and waving a hand in front of Maya's face. "Earth to Maya!"

Maya blinked and looked up. "Oh," she said. "Um, what?"

"Are you okay?" Pia asked her. "You look kind of weird."

"Um . . ." Maya started blinking really fast, and her big, green eyes filled up with tears!

Chapter 3

"Oh my gosh!" Pia cried. "I'm sorry, Maya. When I said you looked weird, I didn't mean anything by it!"

"N-no, it's not that." Maya shook her head. "I'm sorry. I'm just a little distracted, that's all."

Lola sat down and put an arm around her shoulders. "What is it?" she asked. "Are you okay?"

Maya swallowed hard and looked around to make sure nobody else was listening. "I'm okay, but Danny Kaja isn't."

"Oh, you mean how Danny got into trouble with Mrs. Musgrove yesterday?" Cole asked.

"Yeah," said Maya. "See, I know what really happened."

Jesse shrugged. "So do we. We were there, remember?"

"Yeah," Cole said. "Mrs. Musgrove was writing a lesson on the board with her back to the class, and someone shot a spitball at her. It hit her right in the back of the head. She was really steamed."

"You guys told us Danny did it," Lola added. "I still can hardly believe he'd do something like that!"

"That's because he didn't," Maya said.

"What?" Pia widened her eyes. "What do you mean, Maya?"

"When she felt the spitball hit her, Mrs. Musgrove turned around to see who did it," Maya explained. "But everyone just pretended they had no idea. So she went back to writing on the board—but then another spitball hit her. This time on the hand."

"The whole class cracked up," Jesse said. "When Mrs. Musgrove spun around again, her face looked like a volcano that was about to explode."

I shivered. Mrs. Musgrove is short-tempered and yells a lot. It wasn't hard to picture her getting that angry.

"So then what happened?" Pia asked.

"Everyone stopped laughing right away," Jesse said. "Except Danny Kaja. He was having, like, a giggling fit or something."

"Uh-huh," Maya said. "He couldn't stop laughing, so Mrs. Musgrove assumed he was the one who shot the spitballs. She searched his desk and found his little wooden flute in there. She thought he must've used it as a spitball shooter."

I knew which flute she was talking about. Danny had played it in music class a few times.

Cole nodded. "Danny kept saying he didn't do it, but she didn't believe him. So she took his flute and gave him a warning. She said she'd call his parents if he causes trouble in class one more time."

"Yeah, but here's the thing," Maya said. "He *didn't* do it. It was Jackie Bailey—I saw him. I was sitting in the back row yesterday right between him and Gracie Campbell."

"Oh!" I exclaimed. "That makes a lot more sense." Unlike Danny, Jackie was definitely *not* quiet or shy or well-behaved.

"That kid is always goofing around!" Cole added.

Jesse shrugged. "So why didn't you tell Mrs. Musgrove that Jackie did it?" she asked Maya. "It's not like she wouldn't believe you. Jackie is always up to something."

"I was going to." Maya bit her lip again. "But when I started to raise my hand, Gracie leaned over and whispered, 'Don't be a snitch.' And Jackie made a face at me, and I could tell he was thinking the same thing as she was."

"So you didn't say anything?" Lola asked.

Maya sighed. "I couldn't decide what to do," she said. "I didn't want everyone to think I was a snitch. But I also didn't want Danny to be accused of something he didn't do. While I was trying to figure out what to do, the bell rang and I just left with everyone else."

Pia patted her on the arm. "I probably would've done the same thing."

Cole nodded. "Mrs. Musgrove said she won't call Danny's parents unless he does something else," he pointed out. "And what are the chances of that happening?"

"Yeah," Rusty said. "Danny never gets in trouble."

I could tell they were trying to make Maya feel better. But I wasn't sure I agreed with what they were saying. It just didn't seem right to let Danny take the blame for something he hadn't done.

Lola seemed to be thinking the same thing. "I

don't know," she said. "I think you should have said something. Who cares if Jackie and Gracie think you're a snitch?"

"Right," Jesse agreed. "Honesty is the best policy."

"You're right, Jesse," I said slowly. "But I guess it would be kind of hard to speak up while people are staring at you and stuff. Maybe you could talk to Mrs. Musgrove about it in private, Maya."

"Yeah. I could," said Maya. "But I'm worried that Jackie would find out I told. And he can be so foul sometimes."

"Speaking of fouls, maybe we should get back to talking about our song," Pia said, sneaking a look at Mr. Ship.

Lola wrinkled her forehead. "What does writing our song have to do with fouls?"

Pia giggled. "Oops, sorry," she said. "See, I was thinking about basketball—you know, like rebounds and fouls and stuff? Anyway, I was thinking we could make our song about that since we're all on teams." She raised one eyebrow and glanced over at me. "Well, except Amy . . . *so far.*"

"Yeah." Lola grinned. *"So far."*

I smiled weakly, forgetting about Maya's problem as I remembered my own. Was I going to join the Comets, or not?

Chapter 4

"Well?" Pia asked as we all left school that afternoon. "Did you make up your mind yet, Amy?"

"It's now or never," Jesse added. "My dad will be here any second to walk us to practice."

"I don't know." I'd been thinking about it almost nonstop for the past two days, and I still wasn't sure I wanted to try to fill Evelyn's basketball shoes. What if I stunk? "Um, don't you think you should try to find someone who already, you know, knows how to play basketball?" I asked.

"No way," Lola said. "We want *you*! It'll be a blast to all play together."

"And this is a great time for you to ease into the team," Jesse added. "We're playing the Pink Ponies on Monday, and we always beat them.

They've only won one game all season."

"Please say you'll join the team, Amy," Maya begged. "Pretty please with coconut sprinkles on top?"

I giggled. "I don't know. I don't really like coconut that much."

"Okay, pretty please with *chocolate* sprinkles on top," Lola said. "Is that better?"

I looked at her, then at Maya, then at Pia and Jesse. They all looked hopeful. How could I let them down?

I took a deep breath and then let it out. "Okay," I said. "I guess I'll do it."

"Yay!" Lola cheered, giving me a big hug. The others all joined in, wrapping their arms around both of us.

"Go, Comets!" Pia cheered.

"Go, Comets!" I yelled, the excitement starting to chase away my nerves.

When Coach Edwards arrived, I asked to use his phone to call my mom and let her know that I had decided to join the team. After I went back into the school to get my gym clothes, I walked with my friends to Sycamore Street Park. Walking with them felt way cooler than it had on Monday. I wasn't really sure why. Maybe it was because on Monday, I was just tagging along with my friends.

But today, I was part of the team. And it felt great!

❀ ❀ ❀

"This way, Amy!" Pia shouted. "You're supposed to pass the ball. And don't forget to keep dribbling if you're going to hold on to it!"

I froze, clutching the ball in both hands. Which was I supposed to do—dribble or pass? "Um . . ." I said.

"Throw it!" Emily cried. "Throw it now! Jesse's wide open!"

"Sorry!" I called breathlessly. I heaved the ball toward Jesse.

At least I meant to aim it toward her. But it slipped out of my grip too early. Instead of flying across the court to Jesse it went kind of sideways and bounced off Teresa's leg.

"Ow!" she yelled.

Maya ran over and scooped up the ball. "It's okay, Amy," she called. "You're getting the hang of it. Just keep trying!"

But I knew she was just being her usual nice self. I wasn't getting the hang of anything. I was horrible at basketball!

Actually, the practice hadn't started out that bad. Coach Edwards had begun by reviewing the rules of the game and having us practice some basic moves. The first activities had been dribbling and shooting the ball. I could dribble pretty well as long as I stood in one place and didn't get distracted. And I'd sunk a basket on my second try.

Then things went downhill fast. Whenever I tried to run and dribble at the same time, I ended up tripping over my own feet and feeling like Oofus the doofus. We worked on passing next, and I was even worse at that. I could sometimes throw the ball to someone if she stood still, but if she kept moving I had a hard time aiming. And I usually forgot to keep dribbling in the meantime, which was against the rules.

Actually, as it turns out, basketball has a *lot* of rules—more than I ever realized from watching other people play. I think I broke all of them in the first twenty minutes! I could tell my friends were kind of surprised by how bad I was. The three St. Victoria's girls, Taylor, Teresa, and Emily, seemed surprised, too. They had been really nice when they heard I was joining the team. But after they saw me play, I could tell they weren't too happy.

"Good scrimmage, girls," Coach Edwards called out, clapping his hands. "That's enough for now. Let's take five, and then we'll do some more passing drills." As I walked past him, he smiled at me. "You're getting the hang of it, Amy. Just keep trying!"

"Thanks, Coach," I said weakly.

We all wandered off to sit down and drink some water. The St. Victoria's girls sat down together on one of the benches near the court. I thought I saw Emily shoot me a worried look, but I wasn't sure.

"Wow," I said as I collapsed on another bench and wiped my sweaty forehead with my sleeve. "Basketball is a lot harder than it looks. I'll never be ready for Monday's game."

"Don't give up so fast, Amy," said Lola as she sat down beside me to grab her water bottle. "None of us were any good when we first started playing basketball. Right, guys?"

"Right." Maya smiled encouragingly. "And just look at us now."

Pia nodded and took a sip out of her water bottle. It was stainless steel with a baby-blue pattern on it that matched her T-shirt perfectly. "Okay, so maybe you're not exactly Michael Jordan right now," she said with a shrug. "But you'll get better—you just need a little more practice."

"Besides, at least now we won't have to forfeit Monday's game," Jesse added.

Pia giggled. "Yeah. And maybe Evelyn can stop apologizing every time she sees any of us."

I smiled as the others laughed, but inside I felt like crying. All my fears about being terrible on the court had come true.

Soon the coach blew his whistle. The others put their water bottles down and jogged back onto the court. I took my time getting up. Was I really ready for more?

Lola hung back with me. "It'll be okay, Amy,"

she said quietly so nobody else could hear. "You can do this."

"I'm not so sure," I said as I tightened the elastic on one of my pigtails. "I'm starting to think basketball just isn't my thing."

"Don't be silly," Lola said. "I *know* you can do this. After all, you weren't sure you could handle going to regular school at first, either, right? And just look how great that turned out."

She had a point. Being on the basketball

court made me feel a little like I had on that first day of regular school—nervous, clumsy, and unsure of what to do.

"Yeah," I said, smiling a little. "All it took to get over that was practice—and some awesome friends, of course."

"Of course." She slung an arm over my shoulder and steered me back onto the court. "And that's all it'll take this time, too—but only if you're willing to try. So how about it?"

Lola's pep talk made me stand up a little straighter. I was starting to feel better already.

"Okay," I said with new determination. "I'm definitely going to try."

"Now let's play ball!" said Lola.

Chapter 5

"Okay, I think I've got it," Jesse said and then cleared her throat. It was Friday afternoon and we were in music class. "'Teamwork, teamwork, pass the ball; work together, one and all . . .'"

"No, no." Pia shook her head. "That verse should go like this—'All for one and one for all; teamwork, teamwork, pass that ball.'"

Rusty laughed. "Come on, you guys. We've got to decide on the lyrics so we can start practicing. Otherwise we'll make fools of ourselves in the recording studio."

After Wednesday afternoon's terrible basketball practice I wasn't really in the mood to sing about teamwork or passing the ball. Despite Lola's pep talk, I hadn't gotten any better after our water break. If anything, I'd gotten even worse! The passing drills were really hard. I couldn't remember who I was supposed to pass to, and even if I did, I couldn't seem to aim and throw the ball quickly enough or hard enough to get it to my teammates. We kept having to stop and start again whenever we got to my turn, which really slowed things down. I was so embarrassed, I wanted to shrink down to the size of an ant and crawl away.

By the end of practice, even Lola didn't seem that eager to give me any more pep talks. All she'd said was, "I'm sure next time will be better." But she didn't really sound like she meant it.

"Let's forget the lyrics for a second, okay?" said Lola. "I have an idea about some instruments we can—"

"I'm sorry, I'm sorry!" Just then Danny Kaja raced into the room. His jacket was halfway on and halfway off and his papers were falling out of his notebook.

"Hey, Danny!" Rory yelled. "Did you forget

to finish getting dressed this morning?" Rory
is one of the meanest kids in the whole fourth
grade.

A few of the other kids laughed, too. But I
didn't, and neither did my friends. It looked like
Danny was really upset.

"Settle down, everyone," said Mr. Ship. "It's
okay, Danny. Just take your seat."

"I'm sorry!" Danny exclaimed again
breathlessly, his dark eyes wide and anxious.

"I—I—I had a speech therapy appointment this morning, and the therapist was running late. I didn't mean to be tardy, I swear!"

"It's all right, Danny," Mr. Ship assured him again. "You didn't miss much—we just got started. Go ahead and join your group."

But Danny still stood there, hugging his backpack to his chest and staring at the teacher. "I'm really sorry," he said. "You won't tell Mrs. Musgrove I was late, will you?"

"I wasn't planning on it," said Mr. Ship. It was obvious to me that Mr. Ship thought that Danny was acting strangely. "Why don't you just take your seat, Danny?"

Maya looked worried. "I guess he's really nervous about being caught doing something wrong again," she said quietly. "He probably thinks if Mrs. Musgrove finds out he was late to music, she'll call his parents."

Pia shrugged. "You heard Mr. Ship. He's not going to tell."

"Yeah. It's no big deal," Rusty said.

Cole nodded. "You just need to chill, Maya. It's not like *you're* the one who threw the spitballs."

"Maybe they're right," Lola said uncertainly. "I mean, you probably could have said something when it happened. But it's over now, and it's not like Danny actually got punished. So, let's get back to work."

❀ ❀ ❀

That afternoon we had another basketball practice. It was the last one before the game on Monday against the Pink Ponies. I tried my best, but it was really hard to keep up with my teammates.

Taylor, Teresa, and Emily kept whispering together every chance they got. I was sure that they were talking about how bad I was. Worse yet, my friends were starting to lose patience with me. Jesse yelled a lot. Maya shot me worried looks. Pia just shook her head and muttered under her breath. Even Lola was having trouble hiding her frustration—

especially when I threw the ball so far out of bounds that it bounced over to the next court and almost hit another team's coach in the head!

By the end of practice, I was feeling terrible. Joining the team was a mistake—a huge mistake!

"Good hustle out there, Amy." Coach Edwards patted me on the back. "You're showing some improvement. Keep at it. You'll do fine on Monday."

If he really believed that, he was crazy. But suddenly I had an idea. "Um, Mr. Edwards?" I said. "I know

I'm not very good. I'll totally understand if you want me to sit the bench for Monday's game. I mean, only five people play at a time anyway. So you'll only want the best players out there, right?"

He chuckled and shook his head. "Don't worry, Amy," he said cheerfully. "My philosophy is 'everyone plays.' You'll all get equal time on the court." He ruffled my hair. "See you at the game."

Chapter 6

"Oh dear!" My grandfather laughed as the basketball flew over the backboard. "Perhaps I don't know my own strength."

We were at the public courts near our house. It was Sunday afternoon and the park was crowded. Some teenage boys were playing on the next court over. They kept looking over at us. I guess we looked like a funny pair—a skinny old man and a clumsy girl playing basketball together.

"I'll get it, Harabujy," I called as I ran to pick up the ball. When I returned, my grandfather was wiping his face on a towel. He looked pretty funny. He's not very tall, and his basketball shorts hung all the way down to his knobby knees. One of his socks was up and the other was down.

Tossing aside the towel, he clapped his hands. "All right, Amy," he said. "Let's keep playing."

"Okay. What letters are we up to again?" I asked, dribbling the ball in front of me.

We were playing a game called Horse. Every time one of us made a basket from a different spot on the court, we got one letter in the word

"horse." The first person to spell the whole word wins.

"I have H-O-R," he said. "You have H-O-R-S. But I might be planning a come-from-behind victory." He winked.

I dribbled the ball again. Then I lifted it, squinting up at the basket. I aimed, I threw . . .

"Score!" I cried as the ball swished through the net. "I win!"

Whew! Finally I'd done something right on the court. Maybe the game wouldn't be a total disaster after all.

❀ ❀ ❀

But I was wrong. Just because I'd been able to beat my grandfather at a game of Horse didn't mean I was any good in a real basketball game. I was still just as bad on Monday as I'd been at practice on Friday. Actually, I was even worse, since being in a real game against another team was way more complicated. It also made me nervous to know that there would be a crowd of people watching us play—including my family.

They had arrived early to get front-row seats in the bleachers at the edge of the park courts.

"Over here, Amy!" Lola shouted from near the basket, waving her arms over her head. "I'm wide open!"

I had the ball and Lola was jumping around, trying to stay clear of the Pink Ponies player who was guarding her. Meanwhile another Pony player was halfway between us. If I threw the ball to the left, she might grab it. But if I threw it to the right, Lola might not be able to reach that far . . . Before I could decide what to do, the Pony player darted forward and swatted the ball right out of my hands!

"Noooo!" Pia howled from the bench, jumping to her feet. "Stop her, you guys! She's going to score!"

Lola pounded after the girl. Teresa tried to run in from the side. But they were both too late. The Pony player sank a basket, and her whole team went wild. Half the people watching from the bleachers jumped to their feet and cheered.

"That's two points for the Ponies," Maya's older brother Vinnie said into his microphone. He was announcing our game from the sidelines. "The score is now tied."

My heart sank. All my friends said the Pink Ponies were the worst team in the league. And now we were tied!

I looked over at Coach Edwards, hoping he would take me out of the game. Pia, Taylor, and Emily were all taking their turns on the bench—any of them would be better than me—even if they were tired. But the coach just shot me a thumbs-up.

"Remember to pass, Amy!" he called encouragingly.

Teresa scowled as she jogged past me. "Yeah," she muttered. "Like, pass anytime you get the ball. Or better yet, stay away from the ball and let us handle it!"

I flinched. It felt like she'd slapped me. I was so stunned that I couldn't think of anything to say as she jogged forward to take her position.

For the next few minutes, I followed Teresa's advice and just tried to stay out of everyone's way. It seemed to be working because Jesse scored, putting us two points ahead.

Finally there was less than a minute left. Whew! Maybe if I could keep this up, we would be okay.

Our team had the ball. Lola was dribbling near the middle of the court, looking for an opening to get to our basket. But two of the Pony players were shadowing her.

"Who's open?" she yelled.

"Over here!" Maya called. But then another Pony player ran over to guard her. "Oops, not anymore!"

The last two Pony players were on Jesse and Teresa. That meant I was the only one open.

"Coming at you, Amy!" Lola called.

A split second later she dashed to one side and shot the ball at me. As it came toward me I held my breath and tried not to think about all the times I'd missed passes like this during practice.

Lola was really good. The ball came right to me. All I had to do was lift up my hands and catch it.

"I got it!" I shouted as I managed to catch the ball.

"Dribble!" Jesse called. "Pass it back to Lola!"

I dribbled the ball a couple of times. When I looked up, I gasped. There were two Pony players racing straight toward me!

Jesse was still shouting at me to pass. Now

Lola and Maya were yelling, too. And Vinnie was counting down the last few seconds of the game. There was so much happening at once that I got confused. The only thing I knew for sure was that I was supposed to pass the ball. So I flung it away from me—straight into the hands of one of the Pony players!

"Oh, no!" Jesse shrieked. "Get her! Defense. *Defense!*"

But the rest of the Comets were too far away. The Pony player streaked down the court.

"Three . . . two . . ." Vinnie counted off.

The Pony player flung the ball toward the basket from a long way away. It sailed through the air . . .

"One . . ." Vinnie said just as the ball swished through the basket, barely touching the rim. "The Ponies score—they win!"

"What?" I blurted out. "We were two points ahead. Isn't it a tie?"

Teresa was the only one near enough to hear me over the cheering of the Ponies and their fans. "When you shoot from that far away, it's worth three points," she said angrily. "They won. I can't believe we just lost to the Pink Ponies. It's all your fault!"

❀ ❀ ❀

"I'm really sorry, you guys," I said for about the millionth time as we walked into the locker room.

"It's okay, Amy." Maya didn't quite meet my eye. "We know you tried."

"Yeah. We'll get them next time," Lola added.

Pia just smiled weakly, and Jesse stared at her sneakers.

I felt terrible as we changed into our regular clothes. I couldn't blame them for being upset. Losing this game could hurt our chances of getting into the finals. After a few moments of silence, I couldn't take it anymore. "Um, I'm going to take my gym bag to the car and tell my family where I am," I said. "I'll be right back."

I grabbed my bag and hurried out of the

locker room. I took a long deep breath as I leaned against a wall in the hallway. I didn't care about taking my stuff to the car. I just needed to be alone for a second.

But all of a sudden I heard voices. I looked up and saw an air vent that led right into the locker room. I could hear my friends talking inside.

"I can't believe we lost to the Pink Ponies,"

Jesse complained. "Amy has to be the worst basketball player ever! My four-year-old sister could've done a better job!"

"Ugh, I know," Emily said. "I feel bad for her. But how can she be so clueless?"

"Maybe we should have tried harder to find someone else," Lola added.

"Come on, you guys." This time Maya spoke up. "Amy's doing her best. And at least we have enough players to qualify now."

"Yeah, but what good does that do us if we lose every game?" Pia said.

"What if we don't even make it to the finals?" Taylor added.

"It would be totally embarrassing if the Uptown Girlz get into the finals and we don't. Jennifer and her clique would never let us live it down." Jesse sounded really steamed.

I felt a sick feeling in the pit of my stomach and I could feel tears well up in my eyes. I'd known my friends thought I was a terrible player. But somehow it was much, much worse to actually hear them say it out loud!

Turning away, I hurried outside to meet my parents and grandparents at the car. After what I'd just overheard, I didn't want to have to face my friends again today—or maybe ever.

Chapter 7

At first I was mad at my friends for talking about me behind my back. But the more I thought about it, the more I understood why they were so upset. They were right. I was terrible, and it was hurting the whole team.

I spent most of Monday evening trying to figure out what to do. My first thought was to quit. The next game was in two weeks; that would probably give them enough time to find someone else to fill my spot.

Then I remembered what my friends had said before. Everyone who was any good was already on a team. What if they couldn't find anyone to take my place? Then they wouldn't be able to play at all, which might make them even more upset with me. That might be even worse than playing and losing.

"If only Evelyn hadn't sprained her wrist," I muttered. "Then I wouldn't be in this situation."

Suddenly I had a great idea! For the first time since the beginning of the game, I smiled.

❀ ❀ ❀

"Okay, girls." Coach Edwards clapped his hands. "Everyone ready? Let's take a few laps around the courts to warm up."

It was Wednesday after school. The previous morning when I got to school, my friends had asked me why I'd disappeared after the game without saying good-bye. I'd made up a story about my mom being in a hurry to get home. I hadn't said a word about overhearing them in the locker room and they didn't mention how we lost the game. In fact, we'd barely talked about basketball except when we were working on our song in music class.

Now that basketball practice was starting I was ready to put my plan into action. As we started jogging around the outside of the courts, I stayed at the back of the pack, right behind Maya. After we'd gone a short distance, I stopped and yelled, "Ow!"

"What is it, Amy?" Lola stopped immediately and hurried back to me.

I leaned over and rubbed my left ankle. "I

think I twisted my ankle. Ooh, ouch!"

The coach and Taylor came over to see what was going on. He made me sit down while he felt my ankle. "I don't think it's sprained," he said. "Might just be a mild strain or something. You'd better sit out this practice and have your folks take you to the clinic if it still hurts later, all right?"

"Sure." I went over to the bench, being sure to hobble a little so it looked like my ankle really hurt, even though it was fine. I felt a little guilty about lying to the coach and my teammates. But I figured this was for the good of the team.

Lola finished her first lap and jogged over with Jesse right behind her. Both of them seemed concerned when I explained what had happened.

"Are you sure you'll be okay?" Lola asked. "Maybe you should call your mom to pick you up early."

That made Jesse look more worried than ever. "No way! What if she has to drop out like

Evelyn? We'd be short a player again."

"Don't worry, it's not that bad. I'll be fine," I said. "I'll just sit here and watch you guys. I'll probably be okay for the next practice."

I sat out for the rest of practice. Without me on the court messing them up, the Comets had a great practice. By the end they were all smiling.

"Great job, girls!" Lola cried as they all left the court. "Have we got our spark back, or what?"

"Totally! We're going to cream the Ravens at our next game." Pia laughed and high-fived Jesse and Teresa.

I grinned and lifted my hand to trade high fives with Maya and Lola. So far my plan was working perfectly! I still got to hang out with my friends and be the extra player they needed. But I didn't have to feel responsible for making them lose. All I had to do was find enough reasons to sit out for most of the practices and most of the games. As long as I could play a little bit I would still qualify to be on the team. If the twisted ankle stopped working, maybe I could pretend to have a headache or something.

I was sure I could I keep this up. It was the perfect plan!

❀ ❀ ❀

That night the phone rang while we were eating dinner. "I wonder who that could be," my grandfather said, jumping up to answer it.

"Check the caller ID, Harabujy," I said.

But it was too late. He'd already picked it up. He always forgets about stuff like caller ID—he says he's too old for that kind of technology.

"Hello, Hodges residence," he said. "How may I be of service?"

I rolled my eyes and traded a smile with my father. We both always tease Harabujy about the way he answers the phone.

A moment later he covered the mouthpiece with his hand. "It's Mr. Edwards, your basketball coach, Amy," he said, sounding very confused. "He said that he's calling to check on how your ankle is doing?"

My mother glanced at me and then stood up. "Here, let me talk to him." She took the phone. "Hello, Mr. Edwards?"

I felt my heart sink. Setting down my chopsticks, I slumped in my chair. I wished I could slide right off it and hide under the table.

When my mom hung up, she looked concerned. "Amy, did you twist your ankle today at practice?"

"Oh dear!" my grandmother said. "Amy, are you all right? Should we call the doctor?"

I knew better than to pretend I didn't know what they were talking about. But how could I explain it? If there was one thing my family couldn't stand, it was lying. I opened my mouth, but I didn't know what to say. Instead I burst into tears.

"I'm sorry," I blurted out. "I'm not hurt, I promise."

"Then how do you explain that phone call?" My mom looked pretty confused.

"I'm sorry," I said again, feeling awful. "See, I didn't know what else to do. I was so terrible, and my friends were talking about me, and I heard them, and—"

My dad raised his hand as a signal for me to slow down. "Hang on," he said. "Why don't we start over from the beginning?"

A few minutes later, they knew the whole story. "We wish you would have talked to us instead of lying, Amy," my mom said. "Maybe we could have helped."

"I know. And I know I shouldn't have lied."

I wiped my eyes with my napkin. "Anyway, I guess I should just drop out. They can probably find someone else. Maybe from another school or something."

They all traded a look. "Are you sure you want to quit, Amy?" my dad asked. "Maybe if you stick it out and try a little harder . . ."

"No way." I shook my head firmly, shuddering as I remembered the terrible things I'd heard my friends say. "I've made up my mind this time. I'll tell the coach Friday at practice."

Chapter 8

I didn't say a word to my friends about my decision all day Thursday or most of Friday. At first I thought maybe I should—after all, it would give them two extra days to look for a new teammate. But I was afraid they'd be so worried about finding someone new that they might try to change my mind like my family had tried to do. And unlike my family, I would know they wouldn't really mean a word of it. I wasn't sure I could stand that.

So I kept my secret all the way until math class on Friday afternoon. Mrs. Clark divided us into groups to work on fractions, and I got paired with Rusty. By now practice was only an hour away. I was so distracted trying to figure out how to tell the coach and my friends that I was quitting that I missed three easy math problems in a row.

"Hey, what's wrong with you today?" Rusty asked after my third wrong answer. He raised his eyebrows so high they almost disappeared into his spiky brown hair. "You're supposed to be the smart one. How am I supposed to slack off if you're slacking off, too?"

I giggled. Rusty can always make me laugh. "Sorry," I said. "I guess I'm kind of distracted."

Suddenly I couldn't keep it to myself any longer. I had to tell someone what I was planning to do. And Rusty had trusted me with a big secret once. I was the only one he'd told when he couldn't afford to buy his costume for our talent show. I figured I could trust him with my secret now. Maybe he would even have some good ideas about how to tell the others.

"Listen, Rusty." I looked around to make sure none of my other friends were close enough to hear. "Can you keep a secret?"

"Sure," he said. "What is it?"

"Well, you know how I joined the Comets, right . . ." After that, I told him the whole story.

He listened quietly until the end.

"Whoa," he said. "I never thought you were a quitter."

"What?" I was kind of surprised. Rusty was great at sports—I'd thought he would agree I was doing the best thing for the team.

"Winners never quit, and quitters never win," he said. "You don't need to drop off the team, Amy," he said. "What you need is some

one-on-one coaching." He thumped his chest. "And I'm volunteering. What do you say? With my expert skills, I bet I can have you playing like a superstar in no time!"

A glimmer of hope flickered inside me. "Do you really think you can teach me to play better?" I asked uncertainly.

"I know I can!" He smiled. "Come on, what do you say? My team doesn't practice today, so I can come watch you guys this afternoon. That way I'll know what we need to work on."

Could this really work? I still wasn't sure. But what did I have to lose?

"I'll try!" I said, feeling a bit better already.

"Cool!" Rusty laughed and gave me a high five. Jennifer and Liza looked up from their seats nearby and stared at us. Rusty grinned back at them. "I just got an answer right," he called over. "We're celebrating."

"Whatever," Jennifer muttered. I giggled as she and Liza both rolled their eyes and went back to their own work.

"Listen, since I'll be helping you get ready for the WNBA, maybe you could help me with something, too," Rusty said to me.

"Sure. What is it?" I asked.

"It's our song for music class," he said almost in a whisper. "Jesse really wants me and Cole to sing that harmony part, and I just can't get it. You're such a good singer I thought maybe you could help me practice."

"Definitely." I smiled at him. It was nice to remember that I wasn't as terrible at everything as I was at basketball. "By the time we're through, you'll be the world's greatest singer and I'll be the star of the Comets!"

❀ ❀ ❀

When practice ended that afternoon, I was feeling a little less optimistic. I'd played even worse than before.

But Rusty was smiling when we came off the court. "Good job, you guys," he called to the others. He was pretending he'd just stopped by that day to cheer us all on.

As soon as they were out of earshot, he pulled me aside. "Well?" I asked sadly. "Is there any hope?"

"Sure, I mean, it's pretty obvious you have no idea what you're doing out there," he said. "But you do have some potential." He sounded as confident as ever.

"So you think you can help?" A little flicker of hope was back.

He nodded and grinned. "I *know* I can help. We'll start tomorrow morning."

Chapter 9

"Don't stop! Just shoot!" Rusty shouted. "Don't even think about it! I know you can do it!"

I tried to do what he said. Running up to the basket, I flung the ball up without thinking.

Unfortunately, I also did it without looking. It smacked into the bottom of the backboard and came straight back down. I ducked aside just in time to keep it from hitting me on the head.

"Time-out." Rusty jogged out onto the court. It was Saturday afternoon, and we'd already been working for two hours straight. Things still seemed pretty bad.

"Let's try something else," he said. He started dribbling the ball, first on one side of his body. Then he bounced the ball through his legs and started dribbling on the other side. It was pretty amazing. "You stand right there," he said,

❀ 75 ❀

pointing to one of the lines on the court. "I'll stand over here. We're going to practice bounce passes for a while."

I gulped. Bounce passes were really hard. I could never make the ball bounce in the direction I wanted it to. "Um, okay . . ." I said.

He bounced the ball to me. I caught it.

"Don't hold it!" he said. "You're thinking too

much and that makes you hold on to the ball for too long."

I tried to pass the ball back to him. But it bounced off to the side. Rusty ran and grabbed it.

"This time when I pass to you, pretend the ball is red-hot like it was just in a fire," he said. "If you hold on to it, you'll get burned. Go!"

He passed the ball again before I could even blink. As it flew toward me, I imagined flames shooting out of it.

As soon as I put my hands on the ball, I pushed it away. It still didn't bounce quite straight. But Rusty let out a cheer.

"Awesome!" he cried. "That was way better. See? You can do this!"

I still wasn't totally sure about that. But I couldn't help grinning. "Should we try it again?"

"Definitely." Rusty dribbled the ball. "Maybe while we're passing, we can practice our song, too. What do you think?"

I smiled. Instead of answering, I just started to sing. "Teamwork, teamwork, pass the ball . . ."

❀ ❀ ❀

Rusty and I worked really hard all weekend. By Monday I was feeling a little more confident— at least until I got to basketball practice. As soon as I stepped onto the court, Teresa glared at me.

"Are you sure your ankle is better?" she hissed. "Maybe you ought to sit out again."

That made me feel so terrible that I managed to forget most of what Rusty had taught me. I played almost as badly as usual.

"It's okay, Amy," Maya said with a sigh as we left the court after practice. "There's still a whole week until the next game."

❀ ❀ ❀

I didn't go to practice again all week. On Wednesday it rained, so practice was canceled. Then on Friday I had a doctor's appointment after school, so I had to miss practice again. I could tell my friends were kind of relieved when I told them, even though they did their best to hide it.

"No big deal," Lola told me. "I'm sure we'll do

fine at the upcoming game on Monday."

My stomach twisted nervously when she said that. I'd been trying not to think about the next game. It was the last one before the finals, and I could tell from the way my friends were acting that it was important.

I was feeling a little better about my playing. Thanks to Rusty's great tips and exercises—and lots and lots of practice—I could sort of do a decent bounce pass. And when I remembered to relax and focus without overthinking, I was actually pretty good at shooting baskets. Even my dribbling was getting better, although I still bounced the ball on my foot now and then. And since Rusty practiced singing as I practiced shooting hoops, he was starting to sound pretty good, too.

Rusty and I had one last practice on Sunday afternoon, just one day before the game. We started off with some passing drills. My chest passes were still kind of weak, so Rusty advised me to stick to bounce passes whenever I could.

"Now let's move on to shooting," he said. "I'll rebound and pass to you on the three-point line. Just shoot as soon as you get the ball, okay?"

I nodded and smiled. Now that I actually knew what the three-point line was, I kind of liked shooting from it. It was fun to try to make the ball arc up and into the basket.

"Your record so far is four in a row," Rusty reminded me as he dribbled and passed the ball to me. "See if you can match that, okay?"

"Okay." I caught the ball and dribbled it. Then I bent my knees, aimed, and threw.

WHOOSH!

"Nothing but net!" Rusty shouted, jumping up to grab the rebound. "Again. Don't psych yourself out. Focus, and then do it."

I made the next shot, too. And the next. And the one after that.

"Way to go!" Rusty said as he tossed me the ball again. "I think you've found your special spot. Let's go for five!"

"She aims," I chanted. "She shoots. She . . ." I held my breath as the ball left my fingertips. It hit the backboard and swooshed right into the basket.

"She scores!" Rusty howled, dancing around.

He was so excited that he forgot to get the rebound, and the ball almost bounced off his head. "You're awesome, Amy! I bet nobody else on the team could do that."

I grinned, feeling really great. I knew I still had some weaknesses. But now I had some strengths, too, like shooting from the three-point line. For someone who had never even picked up a basketball before a couple of weeks ago, I figured that wasn't so bad!

Chapter 10

I thought about calling my friends on Sunday night to tell them the good news: They didn't have to worry about me dragging down the team anymore! But it was already dinnertime when I got home, and by the time I finished doing the dishes afterward it was too late to call.

Besides, I figured maybe it would be more fun to surprise them. So I didn't say anything about my new skills all day Monday at school, either. By the time I arrived at the gym that afternoon, I was feeling totally pumped up for the game. But I did my best to hide my excitement, not wanting to give away my secret. I could hardly wait for my friends to see the results of Rusty's and my secret plan!

A few minutes after Coach Edwards sent me into the game for the first time, Pia got the ball.

One of the girls from the other team was in her face so much she could barely move.

"Who's open?" she yelled, sounding frustrated.

"Me—whoops, nevermind," Lola called as two of the other team's players swooped down on her.

This was my chance! "I'm open!" I called out. "Over here, Pia!"

I held out my hands, ready to put everything Rusty had taught me into action. *Don't overthink it, just do it*, I told myself.

I knew Pia heard me. She looked right at me. Then she turned the other way.

"Heads-up, T!" she shouted. She shot the ball toward Teresa.

"Oof!" Teresa dove for it, but she crashed into the player guarding her. The ball bounced off both of them and went out of bounds.

I frowned. Why hadn't Pia passed to me?

But I shrugged it off. Maybe I hadn't yelled loudly enough.

However, the rest of the first half went the

same way. Before long I realized the truth. My
teammates were doing everything they could to
keep the ball out of my hands! It was as if there
were only four players on the court instead of
five whenever I was out there. I guess they had a
secret plan of their own to not pass me the ball.

During halftime I hurried over to Rusty. He
was watching from the bleachers.

"Looks like the other Comets are playing

keep-away, not basketball," he said.

"I know." I shot a look at the others. Coach Edwards was talking to Jesse, but everyone else was huddled together at the bench. "I keep calling for the ball, but they won't pass to me."

"Well, they'd better get over it," Rusty said. "The Ravens are kicking your butts so far, and if you guys don't win today you might not make the finals. Maybe you should just tell them about how we've been practicing and how you've gotten better."

Actually, I wished I already had. I bit my lip and looked over at them. I was sure that Lola and Maya would trust me if I explained it to them right now. Well, *pretty* sure, anyway. Probably Pia, too. I wasn't so sure about Jesse. And I was pretty sure the St. Victoria's girls definitely *wouldn't* believe I could play better now. Why should they?

Just then the whistle blew to start the third quarter of the game. "I've got to go," I told Rusty. "Wish us luck."

"Good luck," he said. "You'll need it."

❀ ❀ ❀

We lost Monday's game by four points. While the Ravens were celebrating, our team gathered at our bench.

"Tough loss, girls," Coach Edwards said sympathetically. "I guess we know what we have to work on from now on, huh? You guys need to remember to pass—Amy was open right by the basket in the last quarter and the rest of you didn't even notice. But I know you all did your best, and I'm sure you'll do better next time!"

"There might not *be* a next time," Jesse grumbled. "If we don't make the finals, we're done for the season."

Everyone looked depressed. "We might still make it," Maya pointed out. "If the Panthers lose their game today, too, then we're still in."

I stared at my feet. If only I'd told them about my lessons with Rusty! I was sure we could have won. But it was too late now.

"I told Coach Rivera to call me when that game ends," Coach Edwards said. "Just sit tight—we should know any minute now."

The Panthers were playing at the public high school courts on the other side of the city. The next few minutes seemed to pass very, very slowly as we all waited for the call from their coach. Finally Coach Edwards's cell phone rang. When he hung up, he was smiling.

"I won't keep you in suspense," he said. "We're in! We play the Uptown Girlz tomorrow afternoon in the championship game!"

Chapter 11

"Hi there, Comets." Jennifer skipped over to our table in music class the next day with Gracie and Liza beside her. "I heard we're playing you guys today."

"Even though the Ravens trashed you yesterday." Gracie smirked.

"Yeah. We heard it was really pathetic," Liza added.

Jesse's temper flared. "Just you wait," she said. "You're the ones who are going to look pathetic this afternoon!"

Jennifer rolled her eyes. "Ooh, I'm *so* scared."

I didn't say anything. I was still feeling weird about what had happened yesterday. Why hadn't my friends talked to me instead of coming up with their stupid keep-away plan? The more I thought about it, the more upset I got.

Just then Mr. Ship came in and told everyone to break into their singing groups. Jennifer and her friends went back to their own table. But Jesse still looked mad. Lola and Pia didn't seem too happy, either. Maya just looked anxious. But none of them said a word to me about Jennifer's taunts.

"I think we decided on the final lyrics yesterday, right?" Cole looked around the table. "Maybe we should start practicing."

We all agreed and started singing. Rusty was sounding good, but I wasn't sure the others even noticed. Everyone seemed kind of distracted. Suddenly our lyrics about teamwork sounded pretty lame.

After about ten minutes, the classroom door opened and Mrs. Musgrove came in. "Pardon the interruption, Mr. Ship," she said in her thick Russian accent. "I brought Principal Brewster's birthday card for you to sign."

Both of them walked over to Mr. Ship's desk in the corner and leaned over it. While their backs were turned, a spitball came flying out of nowhere! It hit Mrs. Musgrove on the back of the head.

"Who did that?" Mrs. Musgrove shouted as she quickly spun around. She pointed her finger at Danny, who was sitting with his group near the piano. "You! Mr. Kaja! I thought taking your flute away would put an end to your mischief, but it seems you have not learned your lesson."

"No!" Danny blurted out. He stutters when he's upset, and I could tell he was having trouble getting his words out now. "I . . . I didn't . . ."

Mrs. Musgrove didn't let him continue. "This time your parents will hear about it!" she exclaimed.

I gasped. I'd almost forgotten about the previous spitball incident. Beside me, I heard Maya gulp. As I turned to look at her, I caught a glimpse of Jackie Bailey at the back of the room. He was grinning from ear to ear and elbowing his friend Spencer, who was sitting beside him. Both boys ducked their heads behind some papers so the teachers couldn't see them.

This was terrible! It was pretty clear that Jackie had thrown that spitball. But just like last time, Danny was going to take the blame.

It didn't seem fair, and I wished there was something I could do. But just like in the basketball game, all I could do was watch and feel helpless.

❀ ❀ ❀

"I think I should have said something the first time." Maya looked miserable as the two of us walked from the lunch line to our table. "Poor Danny!"

"Did Jackie really say he'd make you sorry if you told?" I asked Maya.

She nodded. "Yeah. On the way out of music today," she said softly.

Just then we passed the table where Danny was sitting. Normally he sat with a few other kids at lunch. But today he was all by himself. His food was sitting in front of him, but he hadn't eaten a bite.

Maya saw him, too. "Oh my gosh," she whispered. "He looks so sad! Come on, let's ask how he's doing."

Danny looked up when we came over. "Hi," he said in his soft voice.

"Are you okay?" Maya perched in the empty chair beside him. "It wasn't fair that Mrs. Musgrove assumed it was you who shot that spitball."

I nodded. "We all know Jackie did it," I added.

Danny's big, brown eyes looked sad. "I just wish my parents would believe that," he said, his lisp more pronounced than usual. "But they'll never believe me over a teacher. They'll probably ground me for a month!"

When we left his table, Maya looked more upset than ever. "That's it!" she exclaimed. "I have to tell Mrs. Musgrove what I know!"

Chapter 12

As we walked to the courts that afternoon for our final game, Maya told us all about her talk with Mrs. Musgrove. "I told her I saw Jackie do it that first time," she explained. "And that I was pretty sure he did it today, too."

"Did she freak out and start yelling in Russian?" Lola asked.

Maya smiled. "No. I thought she might yell at me for not telling her sooner, but she didn't. She thanked me for my courage and honesty."

"You guys should've seen it when the rest of us got back to class." Cole grinned. The boys were walking with us—both of them wanted to be there to cheer us on in the finals. "She scolded Jackie in front of the whole class and told him that she'll be speaking with his parents tonight.

Then she apologized to Danny for her mistake."

"She gave Danny his flute back, too," Jesse added.

"Whew!" I said. "He must be totally relieved that she's not going to call his parents after all."

Jesse nodded. "Danny's also happy because now he can play his flute at the recording studio and not have to use one of the gross, germy ones from the music room."

"So is Jackie giving you a hard time, Maya?" Pia asked.

She shrugged. "Sort of. He threw some spitballs at me in the hall after school, and Gracie keeps calling me Maya Snitchelloni instead of Maya Vitelloni. But that's okay. It doesn't bother me because I know it was the right thing to do."

I was proud of her for speaking up. I only wished I could be that brave. I still hadn't figured out how to tell my friends about my new and improved basketball skills. I could tell Rusty didn't understand why I was still keeping quiet. But it just never seemed like the right time to bring it up. Besides, I was still mad that they had talked behind my back and plotted against me. As we neared the basketball courts, the rest of the Comets got pretty quiet. "I just hope the Girlz don't beat us by too much today," Pia said with a sigh.

Jesse scowled. "Even if they only beat us by one point, they'll never let us forget it."

"One point?" Lola rolled her eyes. "We lost to the Ravens by *four*, remember? When the Girlz played the Ravens they beat them by, like, ten."

Rusty looked at me and raised his eyebrows. I shrugged and looked away, still not ready to rock the boat.

❀ ❀ ❀

"Five seconds left, Comets! Let's do it!" Jesse shouted as she ran out onto the court. Coach Edwards had just sent her in for Pia.

I wished he would replace me, too. It wasn't like I was getting to play anyway. I'd been in for most of the final quarter, but my teammates were sticking to their plan to keep the ball out of my hands. So far things weren't quite as bad as we'd all feared. The entire game had been competitive and close, with the two teams trading the lead back and forth. But in the last few minutes, the Uptown Girlz had pulled ahead again. They were winning by two points, with only five seconds left on the clock.

"We need a three-pointer to win!" Maya shouted from the bench, clapping her hands. "Let's do it, guys!"

"Fat chance," Jennifer called out with a laugh as she faced off against Lola and waited for the whistle to resume play. "Come on, girls. Time to finish them off. Championship party at my house later!"

The whistle blew, and the game started again. Lola had the ball and started to drive it down the court toward our basket. But the Uptown Girlz weren't letting her get anywhere.

"Pass!" Coach Edwards shouted from the sidelines. "Amy's open!"

Lola looked at me, but then turned and took a shot at the basket instead. The ball bounced off the rim . . . and right into Jennifer's hands!

"Yes!" Gracie shrieked from the Uptown Girlz's bench. "We're definitely going to win now!"

It was obvious that Gracie thought her team had just won the game. But I knew there were still a couple of seconds left. Until the clock ran

out, we still had a shot at catching up.

Focus, and then do it! I heard Rusty say in my head.

Jennifer was dribbling back toward the center. I leaped forward and swatted the ball out of her hands.

"Hey!" she cried.

Ignoring her, I spun around and quickly dribbled the ball to my "special spot." This time I didn't hesitate or wonder what to do. I just launched a shot from the three-point line.

Suddenly it seemed like everything stood still. It was so silent you could hear a pin drop. All eyes were glued to the ball as it soared through the air for what felt like an eternity.

As the ball rattled around the rim, I held my breath. *Please, let it go in*, I thought. Then, finally, the ball dropped through the basket just as the buzzer sounded.

"The Comets win!" screamed the announcer. The crowd erupted in cheers.

The Uptown Girlz stood there looking

stunned. The other Comets on the court with me started shrieking and laughing and jumping up and down. Pia, Maya, and Teresa got up from the bench and raced over, too. All seven of my teammates threw themselves at me, hugging me and patting me on the back. In the stands, I could see my parents and grandparents going crazy, cheering and clapping. They had even brought my dog, Giggles, along in a dog carrier!

"Great shot, Amy!" Coach Edwards exclaimed.

"Totally great! How on earth did you do that, Amy?" Lola exclaimed happily.

"It was Rusty," I said, still feeling kind of surprised myself. "Um, he's been training me for the past week and a half." I smiled at Rusty as he and Cole ran over to celebrate with us.

"Really? Well, you did a great job," Pia declared, her eyes sparkling as she gave Rusty a high five. "That was awesome!"

"Totally," Cole added. "I can't believe you made that shot, Amy! I can't even make those!"

Maya nodded. "We're sorry we ever doubted you, Amy. Who knew you'd be the star of the whole game?"

I bit my lip, backing away from them as my high spirits suddenly sank. Sure, it felt good to hear them praise me. But it didn't totally erase how bad I'd felt before.

"Um, yeah, I know," I muttered. "Look, I knew I was bad. You didn't have to talk about me behind my back and make secret plans to never pass me the ball!"

For a second none of them answered. The three St. Victoria's girls traded a look and sort of

backed away. The others just looked shocked.

"I heard you talking about what a stinky player I was," I added with a frown. "In the locker room that day."

Then I turned away, my eyes filling with tears. The hurt feelings rushed back as I remembered the things they'd said.

"Amy," Pia said tentatively. "Listen, we're really sorry about that."

"Yeah. If we'd known you were listening, we never would've said those things," Jesse added.

"Ssh!" Maya frowned at her. "That doesn't make it any better. We shouldn't have said any of it."

"True," Lola agreed. "We were totally wrong, Amy. We just got frustrated because we wanted to win so badly. Will you forgive us? Pretty please with double chocolate sprinkles?"

There was a moment of silence. I didn't know what to say. Did they mean it? I was pretty sure they did, but could I trust that they'd never do something like that again? I wasn't sure I could stand it if they ever did . . .

Finally Rusty cleared his throat. "Teamwork, teamwork, pass the ball," he sang in a strong, clear voice.

"All for one and one for all." First Cole joined in, then Lola and Maya, and finally Jesse and Pia. "Passing, shooting, it's all fun; but working together gets it done."

I started to smile as I listened to the lyrics we'd written. They were totally true! It made me realize that I *had* to forgive my friends. We were a team, and that was just what teamwork was all about.

I took a deep breath and said, "I forgive you guys."

They all started laughing and babbling at once. I could tell they were feeling as relieved as I was. We all hugged again while the boys kept singing.

Lola was the first to pull away. "Hey," she said. "Now that that's all settled, I just have one more question. Since when is Rusty such a good singer?"

I looked at Rusty. He looked at me. We both

grinned and started laughing.

"Um, actually Rusty and I had a secret plan we didn't tell you guys about yet," I said with a laugh. "Just in time for our trip to the recording studio next week!"

"I wanna hear all about it," said Lola. "But first, let's go ask if we can walk over to Lovem's. I think we all deserve to celebrate with a nice banana split!"

That sounded like a perfect plan to me. We needed to celebrate as a team—and more importantly, as friends!

GO TEAM! ❀

When I decided to join the team!

Our team photo!

My family came to all my games.

Rusty was a great coach!

♡ About the Authors ✿

Kim Wayans and Kevin Knotts are actors and writers (and wife and husband) who live in Los Angeles, California. Kevin was raised on a ranch in Oklahoma, and Kim grew up in the heart of New York City. They were inspired to write the Amy Hodgepodge series by their beautiful nieces and nephews—many of whom are mixed-race children—and by the fact that when you look around the world today, it's more of a hodgepodge than ever.